THE MYSTERY in FLAT 6B

KAREN McCOMBIE
ILLUSTRATED BY THY BUI

BLOOMSBURY EDUCATION

BLOOMSBURY EDUCATION
Bloomsbury Publishing Plc
50 Bedford Square, London, WC1B 3DP, UK
29 Earlsfort Terrace, Dublin 2, Ireland

BLOOMSBURY, BLOOMSBURY EDUCATION and the Diana logo are trademarks of
Bloomsbury Publishing Plc

First published in Great Britain in 2023 by Bloomsbury Publishing Plc

Text copyright © Karen McCombie, 2023
Illustrations copyright © Thy Bui, 2023

Karen McCombie and Thy Bui have asserted their rights under the Copyright, Designs
and Patents Act, 1988, to be identified as Author and Illustrator of this work

A catalogue record for this book is available from the British Library

ISBN: PB: 978-1-8019-9180-3; ePDF: 978-1-8019-9179-7; ePub: 978-1-8019-9182-7

2 4 6 8 10 9 7 5 3 1

Text design by Laura Nate

CONTENTS

CHAPTER ONE

It's been less than an hour since me, Dad and my pet rat Spike ditched our old house and caught the bus to our new flat.

It's in a big, squat block called Seaview Court, six storeys high and as wide as a football pitch.

The whole building looks gloomy, I think as the three of us walk towards it, with Spike peeking out of his plastic carry-case. There's a heavy haze of fog almost hiding the top floor. Our floor, where we'll find our flat. I haven't seen it yet. And Dad forgot to take photos when he viewed it a couple of weeks ago.

"Look, JoJo – the removal team are here already!" Dad says brightly. He nods towards a parked van with '*WE ♥ TO MOVE IT, MOVE IT!*' written on the side. It's a pretty funny slogan and would've made me laugh – or sing it out loud – at any other time, but not today. Nothing seems too funny at the moment.

"OK, now what's the code to get in?" Dad mumbles as we reach the glass doors of the entrance. He's frowning at the rows of silver buttons on a panel. "Let me check that email I got from–"

Stepping in front of him, I drop my skateboard to the ground and quickly press three buttons: '6', 'A' and then 'Enter'. The door clicks open.

"Ah, of *course* the code is just the number of our flat," Dad laughs at himself.

"Yep," I reply, holding the door so Dad can go in first.

Honestly, Dad is super-smart in lots of ways. He was the manager of a whole store before it shut down last year. But he can be super-dumb with obvious stuff, like most adults.

"Right, let's see how the guys are getting on," says Dad.

We see straightaway. There are two lifts, but one has an 'out of order' sign on it. The whole of the entrance area is clogged up with piled-up cardboard boxes and furniture. I spot two men wearing T-shirts with '*WE ♥ TO MOVE IT, MOVE IT!*' on the front. They've just turned our battered old piano on its end, and seem to be trying to figure out how to manoeuvre it into the one working lift.

By the looks of it, the piano will be even *more* battered than it already is once they finally get it into our flat. I told Dad not to take it with us. How many times have I said that I don't want to play it anymore? Not with this annoying twitch I've got going on in my arm. But then I can't just stand here and watch the piano get thunked about. It's making twanging and plinking noises like it's in distress...

"I'm going to take the stairs," I tell Dad, holding Spike's carrier in my left hand and my skateboard in my right.

"Huh? You sure, JoJo? It's a long way up!" Dad calls after me, but I'm already through the door marked 'STAIRS TO ALL FLOORS'.

At first glance the stairwell looks boring and dull – blank breeze-block walls, blank cement steps, no windows and too-bright overhead lights.

"Hello!" I call out, to test the echo.

"Hello!" my voice comes back, sounding odd as it bounces back down at me, sounding higher, more like a girl's.

Me and Spike set off, and quickly climb up the stairs, taking two steps at a time. Floor 1, Floor 2, Floor 3, Floor 4... it's all just the same grey blankness, only broken up by big red plastic numbers beside each doorway.

But half-way up to Floor 5 I see something different. Something scrawled on the wall.

THIS WAY!!!!

I stop dead and stare at the bubble lettering and wonky arrow doodled in peach chalk.

"This way to what?" I say out loud, grinning to myself and talking to no one.

I hear a high-pitched sound like a giggle, but it was probably just Spike squeaking, protesting, feeling travel-sick in his carrier.

Giving myself a shake, I stare at the unexpected words again.

THIS WAY... to the next flight of stairs?

THIS WAY... to a mugger, huddling on the next floor, ready to nab my belongings?

At that thought, my heart begins to pump the words 'RUN, RUN, RUN!' to my brain, but my brain seems to have other ideas. It's remaining perfectly calm, reminding me that muggers wouldn't be interested in a battered skateboard or a black-and-white rat that looks a bit like a small cow.

So I carry on up *another* set of stairs and come across *another* arrow – peppermint green this time.

NEARLY THERE!!!!

I spy a smiley face drawn beside that message.

See? says my brain. *That definitely doesn't sound like something a mugger would do.*

I really want to believe that as I nervously turn around the last bend in the stairwell, where I spot three things...

1) a giant red plastic number '6' on the wall

2) a flurry of the most amazing, pastel clouds chalked onto the wall facing me

3) a girl sitting cross-legged on the landing, with a grin so wide it shows off a big gap between her front teeth.

She doesn't *look* like a mugger. She has long dark hair and is wearing a baggy jumper, denim shorts and beat-up trainers. There's a hole in the knee of her black tights. She's twiddling a pack of chalks between her dusty, colour-smudged fingers.

"Boo!" says the girl.

And like the idiot that I am, I jump.

CHAPTER TWO

The cross-legged girl sniggers. I hate it when people snigger at me. But then she apologises, which is something, I suppose.

"Sorry – I didn't mean to surprise you," she says. Her eyes drop to the carry case. "Oh, wow! What's in there?"

I bumble up the last few steps to the sixth floor landing. I hope my cheeks don't look as hot pink as they feel.

"This is my pet rat Spike," I say.

"Oh, he's SO cute!" says the still-seated girl, her face at exactly the right height to look directly into Spike's carrier. "I've never seen one with black-and-white splodges like that. He looks like—"

"A cow," I interrupt, guessing what she's going to say.

"A teeny-tiny little cow!" the girl laughs. "*Moo...*"

I can see Spike's whiskers poking out of the cage door, sniffing the air, sniffing at this new person.

"I like the, uh, wall..." I say shyly. I point at the chalk clouds with my right hand, which chooses *this* moment to jerk. Luckily the girl's still staring at Spike, and doesn't notice.

"Thanks. Drawing's my favourite thing," she says, while gently stroking Spike's quivering nose. "So, I haven't seen you and Spike around here before. Are you visiting someone?"

"No, we're moving in today," I answer, feeling suddenly heavy with homesickness for our old house.

"Yeah? We live in 6M," says the girl, now springing to her feet. "Which one are you moving into?"

"I think we must be at different ends of the corridor. Our flat is 6A," I reply, hearing the creak, squeak and clunk of the lift door opening nearby, and the muffled, gruff voices of the removal men.

"Oh! Flat 6A?" says the girl, her eyebrows arching in surprise.

What does that mean? I worry to myself. *Is the flat awful? Wrecked? Did someone die in there maybe? Is it haunted?*

"What's wrong with Flat 6A?" I ask out loud.

"Nothing – the problem is the flat *next door* to you," says the girl.

Uh-oh. It's bad enough that we've had to move, especially since I've got to start at a new school after the holidays. But if we end up having nightmare neighbours then that's going to be zero fun.

"So who lives there?" I ask, though I'm slightly distracted by the sound of even *more* voices and clattering out in the corridor. I should go – Dad'll wonder where I am.

"Well, that's the thing," says the girl, widening her eyes. "There's someone being kept hidden in that flat. A child!"

"Huh? Like a hostage?" I say, with prickles of excitement and dread rushing across my chest.

"Yeah! Exactly! An actual hos–"

The stair door is suddenly yanked open.

"Ow!" I yelp as the girl elbows me sharply in the ribs.

But I know what that dig means.

It means I've just met the kidnapper from Flat 6B.

CHAPTER THREE

Hearing that you're about to move next door to a hostage situation is a LOT to take in. And I haven't had a second to picture what a kidnapper looks like.

Turns out it's an older woman with short grey hair and glasses, dressed in ordinary trousers and a navy cardie, pulling one of those shopping bags on wheels.

"It's her!" the girl mouths silently at me, as if I hadn't worked it out. "Mrs Malone!"

"This is ridiculous!" the woman is shouting over her shoulder, while pausing half-way through the door. I recognise her rich, rolling accent; it's Irish. I'm staring at an old Irish lady called Mrs Malone, who is apparently an *actual* kidnapper, according to the girl standing next to me. How nuts is this?

"How on earth are tenants meant to manage with only one lift working and someone's furniture clogging the other one?!" Mrs Malone moans on.

"I'm sorry, love," I hear one of the removal men call out. "If you give us five minutes you can use it before we carry on with–"

"Five minutes?! I don't have five minutes to wait!" Mrs Malone snaps, stepping into the stairwell and letting the door clank shut behind her. She rolls her eyes when she sees us both. "Oh. Is this a youth centre now? Not got homes to go to?"

"It's a bit crowded at mine," the girl says. "My mum's doing my auntie's hair and my little brothers and our cousins are running around and–"

The older woman puts up her hand to let the girl know that's enough.

"He's moving in – right now," the girl carries on, though Mrs Malone has picked up her wheelie bag and is carrying it down the stairs. "He's going to be your next door neighbour!"

"Is he now?" says Mrs Malone, turning back and giving me a stern look. "Well, I hope your family's not a noisy one. I can't be doing with noise."

"I, um, no, I don't think so," I mumble, feeling my cheeks flame again.

"I saw a piano," the older woman announces. "Is it *you* that plays it?"

It feels like I'm being accused of something. I bet Mrs Malone has pianos on

23

a Banned Noise list for being too loud.

"I did, but I don't," I mumble some more. "I mean, I haven't played for a while."

My arm jerks, as if to let everyone know what my problem is.

"Got a tic, have you?" Mrs Malone says bluntly.

"Kind of," I say, feeling self-conscious. What business is it of hers?

"Well, I–"

Who knows what nosey Mrs Malone was about to say, because a certain noise interrupts her.

"Squeet!"

It's a sudden, tiny sound, but I'm very thankful for it. It makes both Mrs Malone and the girl turn their attention away from me and my wonky arm.

"And what have you got in there?" Mrs Malone asks, nodding at the pet carrier.

"It, er, my rat," I say, pretty sure that's not going to go down well. It doesn't.

"Vermin?! As a pet?!" Mrs Malone says, the disgust obvious in her voice.

"It's very cute… it looks like a tiny cow, doesn't it?" says the girl, trying to have my back, I suppose.

"A tiny cow?! Oh, for goodness sake… what nonsense are they teaching you lot at school nowadays?" Mrs Malone mutters, then stomps off down the concrete stairs again. But at the turning down to Floor 5, she looks back and has one last barbed comment to make. "I'll let you get back to vandalising council property."

Me and the girl both turn and look at the artwork on the wall. It's hardly an ugly jumble of spray-painted tags!

"It's just chalk," says the girl, sounding deflated. "It would wash off…"

"Well, washing it off would keep you out of mischief, I suppose," says Mrs Malone, her voice echoing as she disappears out of view.

The girl looks at me, rolls her eyes and motions for me to follow her out of the stairwell and into the long corridor of the sixth floor. Opposite us are the silver doors of the pair of lifts.

"She's pretty fierce," I say, in a low voice, just in case Mrs Malone has supersonic hearing.

"Told you," laughs the girl.

"I mean, how can she not like your drawings?" I say, picturing the beautiful, billowing clouds, and wondering how Mrs Malone could consider them 'vandalism'.

"Some people have no taste," the girl says with a laugh. "But I don't care. All the other neighbours on our floor like my drawings. They say it cheers the place up. Anyway, my flat's this way."

She's waving vaguely to the right, where rows of red-painted doors stand like soldiers on parade.

"That way's yours."

More red doors to the left. It seems like the girl is going to accompany me all the way to the new flat, as if I could get lost in this straight line. As if I can't see half a piano and a huffing removal man at the very end of the corridor.

"So I know your rat's name," says the girl. "But what's yours?"

"JoJo," I tell her, but I forget to ask hers in return, because my head is now whirling.

Was she just fooling around about Mrs Malone hiding someone in her flat? You know, winding up the new kid?

"I'm Daria," says the girl, then breaks into a skippetty sort of run. She does a quick spin as we get closer to 'my' flat, and holds both hands out to the door before it. "And this is Flat 6B…"

I catch up and stare at it. The red door gives nothing away. The silver handle and the letterbox look shiny and polished. Nothing screams 'hostage-taker'.

"You aren't serious about someone being hidden inside, are you?" I ask.

"Of course I am," says Daria, looking hurt. "I first heard the two voices a while ago, when my brother Tomasz ran all the way to this end of the corridor. I caught him right here, and that's when I heard stuff."

"What stuff?" I ask.

"I couldn't make out actual words, but it *definitely* sounded like an argument, and it was *definitely* Mrs Malone and a young girl's voice," says Daria. "I couldn't concentrate 'cause Tomasz was wriggling and shrieking. Then Mrs Malone came to the door, complaining about the noise."

"Maybe she has a granddaughter living with her?" I suggest. "A boy in my old class has been brought up by his granny and grandad–"

"Nope!" says Daria, shaking her head. "Mum came running along with my other brother Jakub and apologised, and Mrs Malone told her that she lived on her own and liked things quiet."

"Did you tell your mum about hearing a girl's voice?" I ask.

"Yes, but Mum never really listens to me – she's too busy and tired with the twins," Daria says with a shrug. "*She* said I was probably just hearing the sound of a TV show. But I know it wasn't that; I've come and hung out *loads* of times since then. And if I hear anything, then it's always the same – Mrs Malone's voice and the little girl's."

My right arm tics a couple of times. This is all a getting bit weird.

Daria turns to me with an earnest look on her face.

"Have a listen through the wall between your two flats. Bet you'll hear something for sure."

"Daria!" a voice shouts and bounces all the way along the corridor. A woman with dark hair is leaning out of a faraway flat. "I need your help with the twins!"

"Got to go," says Daria. "But we'll catch up. Tell me what you can hear."

I watch her go. As soon as the slap-slap of her trainers fades away and I'm alone, I can't help myself. I lean the side of my head against the red gloss of Flat 6B's door, and listen… to silence.

"JoJo! I thought you'd got lost," says Dad, appearing out of the open doorway of our flat. "What are you doing?"

"No, I mean… it's just that I thought I heard a funny noise," I lie lamely. "But it was nothing."

"Well, we'll get used to all the new sights and sounds in no time," Dad says cheerfully. "So, ready to see your new home?"

"Yeah, sure," I mumble, walking away from Flat 6B, with one last wondering glance.

CHAPTER FOUR

Yesterday, the inside of our new flat seemed
as grey and gloomy as the fog outside.
With practically a fort of cardboard boxes
everywhere, the place had felt about as cosy
as the warehouse at Dad's old work. All we
were missing was a forklift truck.

But Dad rigged up his phone and
speakers and we had a playlist and takeaway
pizza to keep us going while we unpacked.
And he denied it, but I think Dad stayed
up the whole night to fix the living room so
it looked more homey. I woke up to see all
our familiar stuff set out: the TV and games

console, the cabinet with all the books and framed photos and Dad's old CDs, the piano all dusted and polished.

"I won't be long," Dad says now as he fastens his tie. "The interview should take about an hour and I'll be back by lunchtime."

I'm not sure how Dad will get on at this particular interview. His suit and shirt are a bit crumpled and neither of us could find the iron.

"The spare keys are on a hook by the front door," Dad carries on. "But obviously you're not going anywhere. Now are you sure you'll be okay, JoJo?"

"Dad, I'm nearly twelve. I'll be fine!" I tell him from the sofa, as Spike runs up my arm and nuzzles into my neck.

"Cool. Well, there's leftover pizza if you're hungry, and call me if you need me.

Promise?" says Dad.

"Promise," I tell him.

He's just about to go when he stops, adding one more order.

"And don't go bursting into next door and rescuing any hostages on your own," he warns, with a teasing grin. "Wait till I'm back with a battering ram and walkie-talkies!"

"Very funny – not!" I call out, just as the front door slams.

Of course I'd told Dad about our new neighbour and what Daria had said about her. And Dad's opinion was that it seems pretty unlikely that an elderly Irish woman would be a criminal mastermind. "I bet it's just a case of a grandchild visiting from time to time," Dad suggested, which sounded very likely and a lot less scary than the story Daria was spinning.

"As if someone could really be hidden away next door," I mutter to Spike, as I stand up to go grab myself some post-breakfast pizza from the kitchen. Spike's little claws dig into my shoulder as he keeps his balance.

But then I find myself wandering over to the space between the piano and the shelving unit. I press my ear up against the plain white wall and strain to hear something, anything.

There's nothing.

With a sigh, I take a step back, and suddenly find myself in a spotlight of warmth as the sun comes out from behind a cloud and beams through the balcony doors. The balcony; I haven't even checked it out yet! There was no point yesterday, thanks to that thick shroud of fog. Now I shove open one of the stiff and screechy doors, and step out to a jumble of noises big and small. Birdsong, the drone of traffic, a football being whacked against a wall, distant reggae from a radio, the chatter of faraway voices, clanks of dishes in sinks, babies crying, someone singing, laughter.

And what about that view!

"Look, Spike!" I say, staring at the whole town spread out in front of me like Google maps come to life. There's the snaking track going into and out of the station. Way in the distance is the high-sided oval of the stadium, and beyond it a sparkle of the sea. I bet I can make out the red brick of my old school on the other side of town. And down there, that concrete, blocky building with the grass all around...

It has to be my new school, right? I think to myself, my tummy twisting in a knot. My tummy twists in an even *bigger* knot when I realise I'm leaning over the balcony, with Spike leaning forward too, sniffing the sixth-floor scents in the air.

"Hey, careful!" I say, grabbing him in my hands and turning round to go back inside.

That's when I *finally* hear something. It's close – it's coming from next door, from Flat 6B.

It's a sound I could recognise anywhere; a piano.

Someone is picking out a tune, haltingly, like they're doing it with just one finger. And then there's a huge clang-clanging racket, as if a little kid has lost patience and is randomly bashing at all the keys.

Now there's a loud voice – Mrs Malone's. It sounds like she's telling someone off, and a kid's voice is answering. A girl's voice. Her tone is pleading, begging…

What's going on in there? Our balconies butt up to one another, with a diagonal cement wall between them, for privacy. But I don't want privacy. I want a chair or a stepladder to stand on so I can peer over and find out who exactly Mrs Malone has in there.

I think quickly, picturing the mess of stuff in the corridor and the other rooms that still have to be sorted. What can I use?

The sudden hammering at my front door makes me nearly leap out of my skin.

CHAPTER FIVE

"Hi, JoJo!" says Daria, practically bouncing on the doormat. "Want to help me in the garden?"

"What?" I ask, wondering what she's talking about. There aren't any gardens around the flats… it's all just acres of concrete and pockets of patchy grass.

"C'mon!" Daria calls out, already doing her skippetty running towards the stairwell door, her dark hair tumbling around her shoulders.

"But…" I bumble, not sure what to do. I don't really know Daria, but I do know I need to talk to her about what I just heard. "Hold on!"

I go back inside the flat and put Spike away safely in his cage in my bedroom. Then I grab the spare keys from the hook and pull the front door shut behind me.

Near to the lifts, Daria is holding the stairwell door open with her well-worn trainer. I can't wait to see her face when I tell her about the music and the muffled voices from Flat 6B.

But as soon as I get out onto the stairwell landing I'm speechless. The bottom of the cloud-covered wall has been transformed. It's like a meadow, made up of weird trumpet-shaped flowers in all sorts of colours, with these huge creepy vines curling everywhere, including on the other walls. It's like looking at an illustration for a freaky fairytale. It's amazing. Stubs of thick pavement chalks litter the grey floor. And it's only now that

I notice the dusty smears all over Daria's hands, T-shirt and even her face.

"Fancy making some plants grow?" she asks, grinning at me and holding out a wide plastic pot full of even more chalks.

"Uh, I'm not great at drawing," I tell her. Mainly because I never know when my right arm might start twitching. I don't say that out loud – I don't want her to notice. I got enough teasing about it at my old school.

"Just colour that one in then," she says, pointing to the outline of something beautiful and sinister.

"It looks like the venus fly-trap I once nagged my dad to buy me," I say. "Only this one's so big it could be a man-eater!"

"I'm training it to eat grumpy old ladies," Daria jokes.

Which reminds me what I have to say.

"Hey, before you came to the door, I heard a piano being played in Mrs Malone's flat," I tell her.

"A piano? I haven't ever heard that!" says Daria. Her face is lit up.

"It's kind of strange, though, isn't it? Mrs Malone seemed to hate the idea of us having one next door to her," I carry on. "And then I heard her sounding annoyed and a kid answering her back."

"Yeah?" says Daria, beginning to bounce on the spot. "I knew it! Could you make out what was going on exactly?"

"No, it was muffled, but I definitely heard the little girl's voice. She sounded upset or—"

Daria holds her hand up to me, mouthing "Shh!" She's tuned into a sound I've missed. A clunk of a door, tap of shoes, a squeak-squeaking along the sixth-floor corridor. The tap and the squeaking stops, and there's a ping as the lift's called.

"It's Mrs Malone – that's her shopping trolley," Daria whispers, while the lift grinds and groans up its square shaft to our floor. There's a swish of doors opening, another as they close… and then Daria's on the move again.

"Where are you going?" I ask, following her out of the stairwell. I see her kneel down outside Mrs Malone's, and I do the same as soon as I catch up.

I guess we're going to listen at the door again, but Daria has other plans. She flips up the letterbox and stares inside.

"What can you see?" I ask.

"Three doors, but all of them are closed."

I picture the lay-out of *our* flat. The bedrooms and bathroom are off the short hallway, with the living room straight ahead. The kitchen is off the living room. Mrs Malone's is bound to be a similar layout, just minus a bedroom.

All of a sudden, Daria stops noseying through the letterbox and does something unexpected.

"Hello? We know you're in there," she calls out. "We're friends – we can help!"

"What are you doing?" I say, alarmed.

"I don't know why I didn't think of this before… HELLO?"

I'm torn between listening and asking questions.

"Daria, what will we do if someone *does* answer?" I ask, my heart hammering.

"I don't know. We'll figure it out," says Daria. "HELLO! Please come to the door if you can."

We wait, our breaths held again.

"I know you're probably scared – but we're just kids too," Daria tries again. "PLEASE let us know if you're there, and if you need help!"

We wait some more.

"If someone *is* there, they're not feeling like they can answer you," I whisper. "Should we just call the police?"

"Nope," Daria answers, shaking her head. "We need more evidence."

"What kind of evidence?" I ask.

"We need to be quick," says Daria, bouncing to her feet.

My chest buzzes with excitement, at the same time as my tummy sinks. What is Daria getting me into?

CHAPTER SIX

I didn't spot the row of shops around the corner when me and Dad and Spike arrived yesterday. They're not too exciting; a launderette, a pharmacy and a mini-market.

We passed the first two and there was no sign of Mrs Malone. But now we're in the mini-market, hiding out at the end of an aisle, the scent of all the racks of spices and herbs tickling our noses.

We've been watching Mrs Malone for a few minutes. She's mostly been frowning at lots of price stickers on things, though she has put a small loaf of bread, a jar of coffee and a bottle of washing-up liquid in her basket. It's not the sort of proof Daria says we need; which means it's not the sort of food you'd buy for a kid you're holding hostage in your home.

I'm starting to feel stupid for being here, and awkward too. The man behind the counter keeps staring over at us, as if he's expecting us to steal a packet of dried coriander or something.

"JoJo!" Daria suddenly hisses. "Look! Check it out!"

Wow – Mrs Malone is actually picking up 'evidence'! A packet of cheesy puff crisps.

"Oh no… my phone's out of battery," Daria groans softly. "Quick – *you* take a photo, JoJo!"

I scrabble around in the pocket of my hoodie. I check in the pockets of my sweatpants. No phone.

"I don't have it!" I tell Daria, suddenly picturing it charging on the arm of the sofa.

Before we left to follow Mrs Malone, I'd run back into the flat to grab my mobile. It only had about 2% battery left, so I quickly plugged it in and texted Dad to let him know I was going out with Daria to the shops. Had he replied? Was he okay about me being out, I wonder? Though it's a bit late to worry about that, I suppose…

And then I feel a hand grab my shoulder and see the shock on Daria's chalk-smeared face.

We're in trouble, aren't we?

My heart pounding, I turn, expecting to see the shopkeeper scowling at me, about to demand I turn out my pockets, before threatening to call the police.

But it's a friendlier face. Sort of.

"JoJo! What are you doing here?" Dad asks, looking a mixture of alarmed and relieved. "I've been calling and calling you but you weren't picking up. And then I was passing and spotted you!"

Me and Dad get on great. I don't like to see him frowning at me like this. And it's not fair – I *did* let him know.

"But I texted you!" I blurt out, with my arm now jerking as if some puppet-master is in control of it.

"I didn't get any text," says Dad, checking his phone screen and shaking his head.

"Look, it's my fault!" Daria bursts out. "My mum needed me to buy some stuff, and I asked JoJo to come with me."

That's a white lie. While I texted Dad, Daria had texted her mum to say that she was going to the shops 'cause *I* needed to get something. And now it's all starting to feel too much of a tangle and my head is pounding.

"Dad, this is Daria," I mumble an introduction.

"Well, I suppose that's okay," says Dad, looking and sounding exhausted. "But please don't ever go anywhere without letting me know, JoJo. Even if it *is* just around the corner for five minutes."

Before I can fumble an apology, someone else speaks.

"Are you my new neighbours, then?" says Mrs Malone, clearly recognising me and now addressing Dad.

"Um, I don't know... are we? JoJo and I just moved into Seaview Court yesterday," says Dad. "We're on the sixth floor. Flat 6A."

"Oh, yes. I'm right next door in 6B and heard ALL the commotion yesterday," says Mrs Malone.

Dad shoots me a look, realising who we're talking to.

"Right, er, sorry if it was a bit noisy," Dad says, before adding "for you... *and* your family."

Dad is asking 'cause of what I've told him, I realise. It's like he's turned detective!

"No – it's just me," says Mrs Malone. "Just the way I like it; nice and peaceful."

She's looking pointedly at Dad, as if she's drilling the rest of that unspoken sentence into his head. *Do NOT disturb me...*

But then I feel as if someone is drilling some information into *my* head. I glance over at Daria and follow her wide eyes as she gazes down at Mrs Malone's basket, where there are the cheesy puffs, and now also a bottle of lemonade and a packet of smiley face biscuits.

See? EXACTLY the sort of stuff KIDS like! Daria is trying to tell me.

So is Mrs Malone lying through her teeth to my dad?

CHAPTER SEVEN

Who knows why there was a tech glitch with my message. Whatever, my text FINALLY pinged to Dad's phone five minutes ago, when we were in the lift on the way home.

I thought that would make everything better, but it hasn't. Dad's definitely grouchy. I understand that he's still rattled from worrying about me not answering my phone, and finding out that I'd left the flat. I think it's also because his interview didn't go so well.

"Don't you think it's a big clue, though?" I say to him, talking about all the kids' favourites in Mrs Malone's mini-market basket.

"How about we just leave it, eh, JoJo?" says Dad, shrugging off his suit jacket and brushing aside the whole Mrs Malone thing. "I know it's fun to make up mysteries, but you said yourself that Daria's mum reckons it's just Mrs Malone watching daytime TV too loud."

"But it's the *same* girl's voice every ti–"

"Look, I've got to jump on this webinar that the employment agency is running," says Dad, looking at his watch and motioning towards his bedroom, where he's set up a tiny office space in the corner.

I don't say anything as he walks away and shuts the door. Now it's *my* turn to be grouchy. I'm grouchy because Dad isn't listening to me.

And actually, I'm grouchy that Dad lost his job and we never have enough money. I'm grouchy about leaving the only home I've ever lived in 'cause we couldn't afford to live there anymore. I'm grouchy about having to change schools. I'm grouchy because I have a feeling that my two best friends are going to forget me really quickly. Not that George and AJ were very good best friends anyway; they were always meeting up and going to the skate park without me. And *they* were the ones who teased me the most about my arm when it started twitching.

What I need to do is hang out with the one true friend I have – Spike. I'm about to head for my room and get him out of his cage when the doorbell rings.

Dad'll have his headphones on and won't hear that, I realise. But then I decide I'm old enough to answer a door and deal with whoever's there. Anyway, it's probably just Daria again.

It's not Daria.

It's some man in work clothes with a clipboard.

"Hello?" I say warily.

"Is your parent or grown-up home?" the man asks. "I'm from the maintenance company."

I don't know what a maintenance company is.

"My dad's on a work call," I tell the man.

"Oh, right. Can you tell him that it's now urgent that we arrange a time to service your combi-boiler? We've had no response to our letters."

I don't know what the man is on about, and don't know what I'm meant to say. But then a door clicks open and someone answers for me.

"They've just moved in," Mrs Malone says sharply. "Give the boy a card with your details and his father will contact you."

I find myself unexpectedly grateful to Mrs Malone for sorting out the situation. I mumble a thank you, take the card that's being handed to me, and go back inside. But it sounds like Mrs Malone isn't finished with the maintenance man *quite* yet.

"So when *exactly* are you coming to mine tomorrow?" I hear her bark at him. "The letter says between 8 am and 6 pm, but I have things to do. I need a set time."

"Well, we don't usually–"

"How hard can it be? Just give me a time!"

I hover behind our front door, listening as the man tries to protest and Mrs Malone wears him down. He finally agrees to send someone to her flat at midday.

"There – that wasn't so hard, was it?" says Mrs Malone as she slams her door firmly shut.

Meanwhile I hover in our hallway, my mind whirling.

Mrs Malone wants a set time for a very specific reason, doesn't she?

She needs to know so that she can lock the hidden girl away from prying eyes…

CHAPTER EIGHT

During school holidays, I usually spend the mornings on my Xbox or hanging out with Spike, cleaning his cage or building him an obstacle course out of whatever's in the recycling bin.

But this morning, I'm drawing bees. Swarms of purple and yellow striped bees, since black chalk doesn't seem to exist.

"They look rubbish," I say, stepping back from the wall and looking at Daria's mad garden.

"They look fine!" says Daria, giving me one of her brilliant gap-toothed grins.

She's drawing dragonflies. That's when she's not darting to the stairwell door and checking on the team of maintenance engineers who are busy bustling from flat to flat on the sixth floor. I've peeked too, and they seem to spend a lot of time propping open the doors to the various flats as they go and borrow tools and stuff from each other. Some neighbours are out chatting in the corridor, while the work goes on in their homes.

It's nearly noon and me and Daria are waiting for someone to head to Flat 6B. When they do, me and Daria are going to hover outside. We're hoping Mrs Malone might go to the shops while her boiler gets checked, and that the engineer will need to go in and out a lot. That way we might see or hear something inside, if we're lucky.

"Listen!" says Daria, suddenly standing tall and still like a meerkat on patrol. "Someone's coming!"

We both drop the chalks and hurry out into the hall, just in time to see a woman with a toolbox go walking down towards Mrs Malone's. We're right behind her, but quickly stop and lean against the wall, pretending to study Daria's phone screen.

"ID, please!" Mrs Malone demands of the woman. Once she's scowled at the lanyard the engineer holds up, Mrs Malone ushers her inside, shooting us a frown before closing the red front door on us.

"We just have to be patient," says Daria, sliding down the wall and onto the cold tiled floor.

"I guess," I mumble, not feeling very patient at all. After hearing more of the piano and the voices when Dad was in the shower this morning, I really, *really* want to figure out what's going on in there.

We wait for twenty long minutes. Mrs Malone doesn't go anywhere. The engineer seems to be very efficient and – annoyingly – doesn't come out to borrow any tools from her workmates. Our flakey plan isn't going to work, is it?

"Hey!" says Daria, suddenly scrabbling upright and dragging me up by my T-shirt. "You've lost your rat, JoJo!"

"What?" I mumble, picturing Spike snoozing in curls of wood-shavings in his cage. "No I haven't."

"Don't worry, that's not a problem," says Daria, giving me a full-beam grin.

CHAPTER NINE

"Yes? What do you two want?" says Mrs Malone, when she opens the door to us.

What we want is to find the girl hidden in her flat. What we want is to have an adult witness – which is where the engineer comes in.

"JoJo's lost his rat!" Daria announces. "Have you seen it?"

My arm is twitching madly, as I get ready for what we're going to do next.

"His rat? Why would I have seen his–"

"There he is! He's just run into your flat!" I lie, as I point into Mrs Malone's hallway.

"Quick, we've got to catch him!" yelps Daria, as we both slither inside the flat, quick as a wink.

"I'll get something to trap it!" says Mrs Malone, slamming the front door shut and rushing off in the direction of the living room and the kitchen beyond.

And with that I dart right, into the bathroom, where I shove aside the dolphin-covered shower curtain. The room's empty. I'm back in the hallway, face-to-face with Daria who shakes her head – the bedroom is obviously empty too. What *has* Mrs Malone done with the girl? Together me and Daria barge into the living room, expecting to see a startled girl sitting on the sofa, who's been warned to stay quiet and act normal in front of the engineer.

But what we find is this...

A living room that has no little girl in it. What it *does* have is lots of cute Lego houses on the shelf unit. And there's even one half-made, on a lap-tray that's been set down on the floor.

"Look!" says Daria, pointing to the glass of bubbly lemonade and small plate of smiley face biscuits on the coffee table. Everything points to a child living here.

And there – there on the TV screen – is an actual child's face; the paused image of a little girl who's scowling at the camera from a piano stool.

"Well, have you caught it?" says Mrs Malone, appearing in the kitchen doorway with a saucepan and a large carrot. The engineer is noseying over her shoulder, expecting to see this missing pet.

Me and Daria are clearly not searching for a non-existent rat any more. We're just standing, staring around the room in confusion. Mrs Malone frowns at us.

"What exactly is going on here?" she asks.

We could say the same to her.

CHAPTER TEN

It turns out that older people are allowed to like lemonade, cheesy puffs and smiley face biscuits just as much as kids. Same goes for building Lego houses. "It's a lot more fun than doing crosswords," Mrs Malone has just told us.

And I've eaten three smiley face biscuits and drunk half a glass of lemonade in the time it's taken to solve the mystery in Flat 6B.

Right now Mrs Malone presses pause on the video we've been watching. The little girl in it got cross and was hammering her fists on the piano keys, while whining to her mum that she wanted to go to the playpark and not do any more boring practice...

"Shelley was only six in this film, and just starting lessons," says Mrs Malone. "She got up to Grade 7 in secondary school, you know."

Shelley is Mrs Malone's daughter. She's now 46 and has been living in Australia for the last few years. Mrs Malone has shown us photos of the grown-up Shelley in her nurse's uniform, outside the hospital she works at in Melbourne. The grown-up Shelley is still recognisable as the little girl in the videos. All the Lego houses on the shelf used to belong to her; they were her most favourite kind of toy.

"I can't believe that we've just been hearing you watching old home movies of your daughter," I mutter.

"Well, *I* can't believe you thought I was holding someone hostage!" says Mrs Malone. "And I certainly can't help it if I'm an old softie and like to watch these videos of Shelley over and over again."

"A softie?" Daria says in surprise. "But you're always so…"

"So what?" asks Mrs Malone, peering over her glasses.

"Fierce," I say, feeling the twitch in my arm start up.

"Fierce?" repeats Mrs Malone, with a hearty laugh.

"Well, to be fair, you are a bit," says the engineer, who's standing in the kitchen doorway with a cup of tea that Mrs Malone has just made her.

"I'm just plain speaking! Either that or I'm messing with people, joking. Why does everyone think I'm fierce?" she asks, looking genuinely confused.

"You always sound shouty with Shelley," says Daria, pointing at the TV.

"Oh, I'm not shouty – I'm just loud!" laughs Mrs Malone. And sure enough, the image that she's paused on has her kissing the top of her whining daughter's head.

Still, Mrs Malone hasn't only sounded fierce through the walls.

"Yes, but that first time I met you on the stairs, you were moaning about our removal men holding you up," I add. "Then you were rude about *lots* of stuff, like Daria's artwork being vandalism, and about Spike being vermin, and about my arm twitching."

Mrs Malone looks taken aback.

"I wasn't moaning about the removal men. I was complaining out loud about the lifts not being maintained," she states. "And I was only teasing about the drawings on the wall and your pet rat. Don't you young people have a sense of humour?"

Me and Daria look at each other and shrug.

"As for your tic, JoJo, I recognised what it was straightaway," Mrs Malone carries on. "My Shelley had a tic when she was young."

"Did she?" I say in surprise. When Dad took me to the doctor, she said lots of people have tics. I just haven't met any yet. It feels kind of good to hear that Mrs Malone understands what it's like.

"Shelley's was right *here*," says Mrs Malone, taping her cheek with her finger.

"It happened whenever she got excited, or worried."

That made sense. The twitching in my arm started when I found out me and Dad would have to move; a time when nothing seemed like it would ever be fun again.

"The doctor said mine is probably 'cause of stress," I tell her.

"Exactly," says Mrs Malone, very matter-of-factly. "Shelley's tic always eased off whenever she played the piano, or played with her Lego. Is there anything that helps *you*, JoJo?"

"I guess hanging out with Spike always calms me down," I say, after thinking for a second.

"And when you've been drawing I haven't noticed your tic," says Daria, through a mouthful of cheesy puffs.

"Yeah?" I reply, picturing the big silly bees from earlier.

Maybe I need to try playing the piano again too. Maybe I need a summer of hanging out with Daria and doing fun stuff and not caring if my arm twitches or not.

"So how often do you go to visit your daughter in Australia, Mrs Malone?" I hear Daria ask now. "Doesn't it take, like, forever to fly there?"

"Never. You wouldn't get *me* on a plane!" Mrs Malone replies with a shudder.

"So do you just talk to her on Zoom or FaceTime or something?" I ask.

"Oh, I can't be doing with technology," says Mrs Malone, waving her hand dismissively. "I'm far too old for that nonsense. No, we just send each other letters every month."

I stare at Mrs Malone's old-fashioned TV and video player as she speaks and realise something. She's one of those people who seems tough and hard-as-nails on the outside, but inside she's a little bit sad and scared, I think. And maybe I can help her, just a tiny bit.

I need to ask someone for a favour first…

CHAPTER ELEVEN

The next day, me and Daria are putting the finishing touches to the updated chalk mural on the stairwell wall.

"How can anyone be scared of technology?" says Daria, bouncing up and down as she examines our artwork.

"Well, how can you be good at *anything* unless someone teaches you how to do it first?" I reply, thinking Daria's not being totally fair to Mrs Malone. "Anyway, shush – she's coming."

Dad's been showing Mrs Malone how to work Zoom on his laptop. He's offered to lend her his computer once a week, so she can have a proper catch-up with Shelley. But since this has been the first time, he's had to promise to sit by Mrs Malone's side, all the way through the chat with her daughter, as Mrs Malone has been worried that the 'picture' might 'disappear', or that she'll press the wrong button and make the laptop explode or melt or something.

"So, what's all this about then?" says Mrs Malone, coming through the stairwell door. "You two vandalising council property again?"

It's a joke. We know she's joking, and yet the smile slips from her face when she sees what we've been doing, and is replaced with an open-mouthed wow of surprise.

The sixth floor stairwell landing of Seaview Court has become an Australian rainforest. Me and Daria went online and found all these brightly coloured plants they have in Australia, and added them into our weird garden. And in amongst the gum trees with pink flowers, and red bottlebrushes and spindly spider flowers, we've drawn kookaburras and lorikeets, wallabies and wombats.

"Well, this is quite something," says Mrs Malone, nodding slowly, taking it all in.

In fact, it's all a bit wonky and not quite in scale, but Daria and me decided that doesn't matter. The point is to make Mrs Malone happy, and from the way she's now dabbing at the corner of her eyes, I think she is.

My phone suddenly pings. It's a message from Dad.

'Don't be long… the jacket potatoes are nearly done!' says the text.

Dad's invited Mrs Malone and Daria for lunch. Afterwards, I've promised to play something for Mrs Malone on the piano. I had a bit of a practice this morning, and luckily my fingers seem to remember what to do. A couple of keys are a bit out of tune after the wrestling match between the piano, the removal guys and the lift the other day, but hopefully no one will notice. My arm twitch behaved too. Like Mrs Malone says, tics seem to calm down when you're concentrating on things you like to do. And maybe I'll like living up here, near the clouds and the birds, with the faraway view of the sea and two new friends I hadn't expected to find so quickly. And don't get me started on the fact that one of my new friends is more than sixty years older than me!

"Dad's texted – food's ready," I tell Daria and Mrs Malone.

Daria spins round and hauls the stairwell door open.

"Hold on," says Mrs Malone. "Is that supposed to be a kiwi?"

She's pointing at a funny-looking round bird with a spike for a beak and no wings.

"Yes!" me and Daria say at the same time, delighted that she's recognised it. So much for me being rubbish at drawing!

"They're native to New Zealand, not Australia!" bellows Mrs Malone. "Honestly, what *do* they teach you children at school these days?!"

She pats us both on the shoulder, and the three of us head off together, our laughter bouncing around the walls of the sixth floor.

READING ZONE!

QUIZ TIME

Can you remember the answers
to these questions?

1. What had the letters and arrows in
the stairwell been drawn with?

2. What word does Mrs Malone use
to describe Spike when she first
meets him?

3. What shops are in the row around
the corner from JoJo's flat?

4. What does Mrs Malone insist the
maintenance man tells her?

5. What was the surprise that
JoJo and Daria created for
Mrs Malone?

READING ZONE!

GET CREATIVE

At the end of the story JoJo and Daria decorate the stairwell to reflect the plants and animals of Australia.

Can you carry out some research to identify what these plants and animals are and then draw a picture of your own?

You could choose a different country to research and draw another design to reflect the plants and animals of your chosen country.

READING ZONE!

WHAT DO YOU THINK?

The character of Mrs Malone appears to change during the story. Do you think her initial behaviour was friendly? Why/why not? How did the relationship between Mrs Malone, JoJo and Daria change? Have you ever met somebody who you thought was grumpy or scary to begin with but once you got to know them they were different?

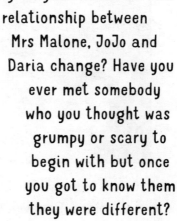

Look out for more books in the
BLOOMSBURY READERS SERIES

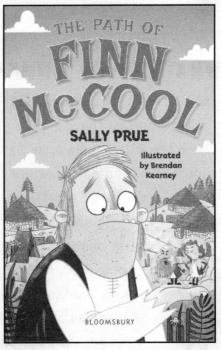

Finn McCool is a giant: the biggest giant in
the whole of Ireland. However, when he sets out
across the sea to Scotland, he realises he isn't
the biggest giant in the world. Soon it's up to
Finn's wife, Oona to come to the rescue.